After Love

Healed

A journey into their lives After Love Heals

Volume II

Written By

Inez S McRae

Forward

The Love of God is fervent in the hearts and minds of those who know him. When we stand on and study the word of God, he shall protect us and direct us.

Ephesians 6: 10-14

[10] **Finally my brethren, be strong in the Lord, and in the power of his might** [11] **Put on the whole armor of God, that ye may be able to stand against the wiles of the devil** [12] **For we wrestle not against flesh and blood, but against principalities, against powers, against the rulers of the darkness of this world, against spiritual wickedness in high places** [13] **Wherefore take unto you the whole armor of God, that ye may be able to withstand in the evil day, and having done all, to stand** [14] **Stand therefore, having your loins girt about with truth, and having on the breastplate of righteousness**

KJV - King James Version

Dedication

This book is dedicated to my church, Macedonia AME, Pastor, Rev. C. Scott, First Lady Dr. C. Scott, Mother Norris, Mother Morris, Mother Mallory, Sis. Armenta Jones, the Golden Jewels, and to everyone who inspired me to write Volume II of this amazing story, " After Love Healed" I hope everyone who reads this novel will enjoy reading it as much as I enjoyed writing it.

Best wishes
Inez Shack-McRae

We may never know how deeply someone carries past pain and hurt... But every once in a while, we're given the opportunity of seeing into another person's heart, that inner glimpse of a woman's heart and soul, only to realize she pulled you in instinctively, only to heal your heart too.

After Angela and Damenian's Christmas Eve wedding ceremony, everyone gathered at Damenian's parents' home. Still in their wedding attire, the newlyweds danced to one love song after another in the middle of his Parents' den. Damenian whispered in Angela's ear, "I love you, Ange. Thank you, Baby, for the best day of my life." Angela kissed Damenian on his neck just below his earlobe, and she whispered, "I love you, Dame, I always will, thank you, Baby, for letting me love you."

The next morning, Christmas Day, they arrived early for his parents' family Christmas festivities. Angela felt surrounded by love and warmth as she shared the holiday with Damenian and his family. For Damenian, it was the first time in years he was home for Christmas, and now, for the first time, he was with a wife by his side.

Damenian planned a two-week honeymoon with Angela beginning the day after Christmas, on December 26th. They would be exploring three international countries where Damenian oversees his company's investments. Damenian, a Senior Executive, manages his company's international investments division; he likes visiting the international team in person. He enjoyed spending time with them, addressing concerns he had for them and concerns they had for him in Dubai, Indonesia, and Thailand.

Damenian had fallen so in love with Angela. He knew, without doubt, she loved him, not for his resources, hefty salary, or any of the privileges to be gained. He knew unequivocally she loved the character in him; she loved him; he thanked God for that and for her. Before meeting Angela, Damenian could ask a woman to have dinner with him, and they went to dinner, no big deal. But with Angela, it was different; it took nearly two years before she eventually went out with him. He thanked God that she is now happily married to him and is the perfect mate for him.

Damenian planned a honeymoon to explore cultures that were new to Angela. He could hardly wait to see her amazement and hear her questions about these fine people, their culture, and their differences and similarities. He was excited and looking forward to spending time internationally with her.

First stop for the honeymooners was Dubai for 5 days, and at least a 4-hour meeting for Damenian to be updated with the international investment trajectory. The rest of his time will be spent in Dubai with his newlywed wife. While in Dubai, they shopped, laughed, dined, and explored the people's culture together. Angela noticed everywhere they went, people knew Damenian and addressed him Good day, Mr. Hammonds. Angela asked Damenian what's going on, and how do so many people know you here? He responded, "I've spent a few years here overseeing my firm's investments, and I also created a lot of jobs for the people here."

Angela immediately put her arms around Damenian and said, "Baby, give me some sugar." He responded by kissing her phenomenal lips quite passionately twice, then Angela said to him, "Is that all the sugar you got for me, Damenian?" he took a step back, chuckled, grinned, and admired his beautiful, phenomenal wife. He extended his hand to her, and she placed her hand in his. She was immediately mesmerized by how much she loved him. Holding hands, they went back to the suite for the duration of the evening.

Next stop Indonesia for 4 days, followed by a 3-hour meeting with Damenian's international team. While in Indonesia, they spent their time among the people, in the street markets, shopping, dining, exploring, and watching people preparing street food on the actual streets for tourists. The aromas smelled like heaven was cooking.

Damenian was fascinated by how Angela wouldn't let him sample foods she had no idea what it could have come from or what it could be, especially if it was prepared with the head and hoofs still attached. She would say, "No, Damenian, I don't know what that could be, baby, we cannot try that, okay," always lovingly with her arms around him. Not many people could or would tell Damenian Hammonds he could not have something. But with Angela it felt different, it felt like love, it felt like someone cared about him, it felt like a real sense of protection mode from Angela, he loved it, he loved her, he even thought it was quite humorous; primarily because no one had ever cared about him like that before, so if Angela said No, he didn't.

Their final destination was Thailand to round out their 2-week honeymoon. Angela felt her best cultural experience was when they were there. Angela felt they were completely honorable people, and their humbleness was truly amazing. Like before, everywhere they went, people greeted Damenian with hello good day Mr. Hammonds. Angela asked Damenian, "Did you create jobs here, too?"

Damenian responded, "Oh yes, I created more jobs here in Thailand than in the other two international divisions I oversee." During their time in Thailand, they loved, laughed, talked endlessly, shopped, and dined.

Damenian sat at their patio table outside, underneath a patio umbrella, and checked his emails and voicemails while Angela shopped in the merchant store with his credit card. He had already made her an authorized user, allowing her to buy whatever she wanted. Angela purchased a few graphic-designed artwork pieces she wanted to use to decorate Damenian's office and their home. After making her décor choices, she had to go back to their patio table outside to retrieve Damenian so he could give the merchant the shipping instructions where he wanted to have her purchases shipped to.

As Angela was approaching Damenian from behind his seat, a woman sat down in her chair directly across from him. She was your average-looking female, nothing strikingly beautiful. So, Angela slowed her pace to linger so she could hear what was being said. Damenian said to the woman, "Excuse me, can I help you with something, Ma'am? That seat is being occupied by my wife; you'll need to get out of her chair." The woman said to Damenian, "I apologize, I saw you sitting here alone, and since I hadn't run into you in a lot of years, I thought".

Damenian cut her off and said, "Ma'am, Ms. Oneka right"? She said yes, that's right, Damenian said, "a seat, any seat that is across from me is permanently occupied for the rest of my life by my wife, so as I stated, you'll need to get out of; before he could say another word, Angela had walked up to the table and into view.

Damenian is so in love with Angela that he's mesmerized by her; you can see it in his eyes whenever she walks into the room or into his view. Angela is the most phenomenal woman he has ever encountered, and her phenomenal beauty has captured his heart as if he were under a spell he never wanted to end. The woman occupying Angela's seat saw the look in Damenian's eyes and knew without doubt that was his wife. Angela introduced herself, she said, "Hi, my name is Angela Hammonds." The woman sat there, unable to reply or speak, as if she was scared right down to her bones.

The woman knew right then, in that very moment, she shouldn't be sitting there; she thought, he is on his honeymoon, and this beautiful woman is his wife. Damenian said, "Angela, this is Ms. Oneka, and Ms. Oneka, this is my wife, Mrs. Angela Hammonds". Damenian said, "Angela, I once asked Ms. Oneka to have dinner with me once, one and a half times many years ago, too soon after my divorce, actually. I realized during dinner with this young lady that this was not going to work for me.

When we finished our meal, the dinner ended. I thanked her for her company and for having dinner with me, I paid the bill and left. Angela, this woman began to blow up my phone the very next day while I was in a very important meeting". Angela started laughing so hard she had to turn her back so the woman couldn't see her laughing her heart out.

Damenian said she left me 6 different voicemails. I deleted every one of them without listening to them. I called her back, and I asked her to meet me for dinner again. I wanted to be unmistakably clear with this young lady as she looked me straight in the eyes. I asked her to let me see her cell phone, I asked her to pull up my contact information, and when she did, I deleted the hell out of it. I was clear with her about the gravity of ever contacting me again. I asked for the check, and I left. I hadn't heard or seen this young woman again until today, Angela.

At that moment, two security personnel dressed in dark clothing approached the table and asked if everything was okay over here, Mr. and Mrs. Hammonds. Damenian said, "It is." They said congratulations once again and enjoy the remainder of your honeymoon here. Angela replied, "Thank you very much," before she turned to Ms. Oneka and said to her, "Have a good night, Ms. Oneka who felt relieved to be dismissed to go. Angela gave Damenian his credit card back, which he put in his wallet.

Holding her hand, after kissing it, they headed back into the merchant store so Damenian could give the merchant delivery instructions to have Angela's purchases shipped to the US. He arranged for all of Angela's purchases to be sent to his international office, then shipped to his U.S. office before being delivered to their home.

Angela soon learned that whenever she needed something, all she had to do was tell Damenian. He would get on the phone, announce himself, Damenian Hammonds here, and the item would be shipped either to his house or his office, with an

(ETA) estimated time of arrival provided. Angela soon learned she could have whatever she needed the same day if she went to Damenian, and she loved it! Angela once tried to place an order for an item and was told there was up to a 9-month waiting list. She told Damenian, who got on the phone with someone and was given an ETA delivery in 2 hours.

Angela began to learn more about Damenian, the things only time will reveal. She cherished every one of his secret vulnerabilities, the ones he would never let his

guard down enough for everyone to see. Damenian had always longed for someone he could love enough, just enough, he could show them his heart in intimate and private moments. Angela, on the other hand, wanted to be a good helpmate and wife to Damenian; she wanted him to instinctively know she loves him; she wanted him to instinctively know she got him, and she's not letting go. Lastly, she wanted him to instinctively keep his eyes on the Lord God and on her.

During their 2-week honeymoon, Angela conceded what she actually knew about Damenian. Besides being an intelligent God-fearing man, he spoke a couple of languages, and he was her hardworking man who needed to be held occasionally, who also needed to be told "I love you" just so he could say it back.

He never had any of that before Angela, so he remained quite mesmerized by her; you could see it in his eyes whenever she walked into the room. Angela's "give me some sugar" never got old with him and actually became both of their go-to phrases to one another. A girl out of (PSP) Prince Street Projects has mesmerized and captured Damenian Hammonds' heart and is now his wife.

Angela never sought Damenian for monetary reasons; she actually didn't have a knowledgeable value of his worth, and she didn't want it. She was content with loving him, being his wife, and just knowing he had a good job, and that was enough for her. Damenian didn't concern his self with the pettiness of knowing Angela's financial stability to run her business successfully since she had never come to him for his help. He knew firsthand that God had blessed Angela and how proud he was to be her husband.

Damenian, a faithful man who serves God, had been taught to keep his eyes on the Lord no matter where this life finds him. He trusted God when the storms came into his life. He kept his eyes on God as taught to him by his father, with whom he had always had a very close relationship. Although he didn't make it home often over the years, he frequently made calls to and from his dad and, over the holidays, to his Mom and sister Ava.

Damenian reminisced about the moment he saw into Angela's heart as she cried in painful grief in the vestibule area of the church. A simple touch from a cold, wet hand towel placed on the back of her neck changed everything. Through it all, they discovered love for one another that was bigger than the two of them. They could relax and be themselves with one another like never before with anyone else. They would talk for hours, laugh, hug, kiss, shop, trust, and enjoy their life together because they loved each other.

There was so much more Angela and Damenian would discover about one another. Angela discovered her husband is a 6th-degree black belt in Taekwondo martial arts. In Korean culture, he is "Roku-dan," which signifies his 20 years as a black belt master of the art, signifying his ability to teach and train others. Damenian taught the discipline of the Taekwondo martial art at one time before he immersed his self totally in work. Angela found herself quite intrigued when he told her his dad is a Brazilian Jiu-Jitsu 10th degree black belt and a 10th degree black belt in Taekwondo. He said, "My dad is 'Kwan Jang Nim,'" a high rank in martial arts, which means "Grand Master," earned by many years of training and experience.

Damenian said, "My dad is up at sunrise every morning practicing his martial art, actually every morning except Saturdays and Sundays because Mom won't let him." I always knew where to go if I needed my dad five out of seven days a week. Angela loved the sparkle she saw in Damenian's eye when he spoke of his father. She wondered how many of those sunrise mornings he might have gone there to his father. She assumed it was as many times as he needed him.

Home After the Honeymoon

Damenian and Angela are back from their Christmas Eve wedding at his parents' church, their Christmas Day festivities at his parents' house, and their two-week international honeymoon. They returned to Damenian's house and Angela's new home.

Angela focused on making her new home with Damenian cozy, warm, and representative of both their personalities. She loved to decorate; she had a strong eye for details, décor, and color palettes. She used her artistic, God-given talent to transform Damenian's bachelor's home into a home for him and her, incorporating the décor she had purchased during their international honeymoon.

She forewarned Damenian that she planned to decorate his office soon. He responded as he normally does, "Okay, Babe, anything you want!"

The one thing Damenian found out about his newlywed wife is she's a homemaker and she loves to cook! Damenian went into his secret place where we all go to commune with God, and he said, "Lord Father God, *she cooks*, Father God, thank you Father." Damenian soon discovered he loved coming home from work to the aroma of something delicious being cooked for dinner by his phenomenal wife.

Angela kept Damenian hands-on during their meals. He was responsible for carving the meat that had been cooked so he could place it on a serving platter for the two of them. If Angela made a roast or his favorite tomahawk steak dinner, he carved. Once he carved a roasted hen by removing the wings and legs, then butterfly-splitting the breast before placing the carved poultry on the dinner platter for the two of them. Whenever Damenian joined her in the kitchen, helping while she prepared dinner, filled Angela with an overwhelming sense of happiness and joy.

Angela had Damenian's office painted a very pale soothing color yellow. She purchased him a huge mahogany desk and a high-back upholstered chair. She brought man-friendly plants 5ft. to 6ft. tall. It was his 5-foot-tall cactus plant that was the conversation piece when anyone entered his office. Angela had purchased a couple of huge abstract graphic art paintings for his office while they were overseas on their honeymoon. For the rear area of his office, she purchased a mahogany conference table that seated 8 comfortably with high-back lamb skin chairs for meetings with his team.

Damenian fell in love with his office; he absolutely, truly loved it. But most of all, he loved the lifestyle changes Angela continuously made around him and her. Damenian was loving every bit of married life with Angela, but he did not want her days filled with cleaning, cooking, laundry, and managing her business. He did not want her to be consumed with all of that. He talked to her about having someone come in a few hours a day to help her with everything, and she agreed, so he called Ms. Sonia.

Ms. Sonia is a God-fearing, praying Christian woman who came a couple of times a week to Damenian's home before and after his divorce. When Damenian called Ms. Sonia, she was so happy and delighted to hear from him. She asked him, "You been okay, Mr. Hammonds, you been taking care of yourself?" Damenian laughed and said, "Yes, Ms. Sonia, I have, I'm actually better than ever. The reason for my call is I got married recently." He said to her, "Oh yes, Ms. Sonia, she is very beautiful, yes ma'am, I am aware you didn't like the other one." Then he said, "No, Ms. Sonia, I couldn't play hard to get because she did. Anyway, we got married on Christmas Eve at my parents' church."

Ms. Sonia, you see my wife, Angela, is a homemaker; she cooks, decorates, cleans, does laundry every week, and runs a successful business. I need someone to come in a few hours a day to help her with some of these things. If you're available, I would like you to meet Angela. Yes, tomorrow morning at 10:30 would be good. He said, "You as well, Ms. Sonia. God bless, see you in the morning."

Ms. Sonia and Angela had chemistry between them. Immediately after meeting each other, they truly liked one another tremendously. Angela made it clear to Ms. Sonia that she would be her assistant and not here to do her chores for her. Angela thought that because she loved to bake and roast in the oven quite frequently, she could really use Ms. Sonia's help. Helping her to keep up with oven cleaning, dropping off orders, etc., would give her plenty of time to comfortably make dinner. She smiled with gratitude when she thought about how thoughtful Damenian was to have thought about doing this for her.

They agreed Ms. Sonia would come to help Angela from 10:30 to 3:00 unless she had a doctor's appointment or planned to go to bingo that day. When Ms. Sonia met Angela, she said to herself, Mr. Hammonds went and married his self an angel that can cook. "Truly, God is blessing Mr. Hammonds." Ms. Sonia felt fortunate and grateful to be a part of Mr. Hammonds' household this time. She had to laugh to herself, though, when she thought Lord, have mercy, Mr. Hammonds got himself a new wife who can cook!

As time passed, Angela would get up a little early to make breakfast for Damenian, and on days she wanted to sleep late, she would tell him to fix a bowl of cereal with an English muffin or a bagel. Angela kept all of his favorite cereals stocked in the pantry: Honey Nut Cheerios, Cap'n Crunch, Frosted Flakes, and Raisin Bran. Usually, if Damenian had to fix himself a bowl of cold cereal for breakfast, Angela would usually make him a nice dinner that evening.

As the weeks and months passed, Damenian and Angela both kept their eyes on God. They attended church together every Sunday, unless they were away at Damenian's parents' house for the weekend. In that case, they would attend his parents' church before heading home. Angela was so grateful and thankful to have Ms. Sonia to help her. She didn't want to alarm Damenian that she was sick most mornings, so she put on a good face until Ms. Sonia got there with the crackers and ginger ale to help her with the nausea.

She told Ms. Sonia she may have caught some kind of bug during her honeymoon, traveling through all those countries. Angela said I don't know how much longer I can keep this from Damenian, since I've been feeling sick a lot lately. Ms. Sonia has always been a comforting woman who encouraged everyone. Angela thought, no wonder Damenian thought of getting her to help her with things and the business.

Ms. Sonia said, "Ms. Hammonds, you need to see a doctor; you really need to know exactly what is wrong with you. Mr. Hammonds, if he finds out something is wrong with you, he'll find a way to fix it." Angela said, "You're right, Ms. Sonia. I'll make an appointment for tomorrow. Please don't say anything to Damenian; he's working on a project at work that means a lot to him. I don't want to distract him from that unless I know what's happening with me." Ms. Sonia promised she would not say anything to Mr. Hammonds.

Immediately, Ms. Sonia thought to herself, "Ms. Hammonds, you're pregnant, baby, you look to be 4 ½ months, nearly 5 months pregnant to me, and you're carrying in the front, that means you're having a boy. She thought, the day I met you Ms. Hammonds I dreamed about fish that same night. (Dreaming about fish is an old wise' tale meaning someone is pregnant.) Ms. Sonia thought, Oh my Lord God, Mr. and Ms. Hammonds don't know they're having a baby. Ms. Sonia immediately prayed a fervent silent prayer of protection over Angela and Damenian. She praised and thanked the Lord for the grace that had led her to be here to help this God-fearing man and his beautiful, angelic wife, who is having his baby.

Angela got away with one more morning being sick and needing Ms. Sonia to bring her crackers and ginger ale.

Meanwhile, Damenian was in such a good space he was happier than she remembered. It seemed the project he was working on was progressing well. Angela knowingly understood that whenever Damenian was working on a project of magnitude, she tried not to distract him unnecessarily. He, on the other hand, had begun to realize most mornings he would be at work when she got up, and often he'd get home some evenings after she'd gone to sleep. So, he thought he'd take her on a trip, a dinner date to catch up on some needed R & R together since the project began to look like it was wrapping up and would be finished soon.

When Damenian began to swiftly move through the ranks of Senior Management to oversee three international divisions, it was accompanied by huge salaries, corporate benefits, and corporate privileges. His parents prayed fervent prayers of protection around their son against what some of these privileges could and would attract if not sent by God. Not so surprisingly, Damenian never brought a woman home to meet his parents until he got engaged to Angela. Damenian's family never had a relationship with anyone Damenian dated or married previously.

Angela, on the other hand, had an amazing relationship with Damenian's family. She loved them, and they loved her. She called his mother "Mom" she called his father "Dad" she adored his sister Ava and Myron her husband who gave the best hugs, always lifting her up off the floor while she would tell him to put her down before he hurt his back as she always called for Ava while Damenian sat there chuckling, shaking his head in joy with amazing love for his family and his wife.

Angela got dressed for her doctor's appointment and planned to do a little farmers' market shopping while she was out. She was heading for the door when Damenian wrapped her in a loving hug with both arms around her. He kissed her and asked her what she'd be doing today. She said a little shopping for the house and dinner tonight. He reached into his wallet and gave her his credit card, the one he made her an authorized user of. Angela thought if you make a person an authorized user, you give them their own card to use, but not her husband, Damenian. She recognized his *need to control,* which was no problem with her.

She said to him, "Babe, I have money, and sometimes I can pay for things." Damenian spoke to her in a tone when he said to her, "I take care of you, Angela. Your money is your money for you, for your business. I work my tail off to marry a woman I can pay for things I couldn't always pay for, because I didn't have this kind of relationship. Now that I can buy whatever you want, you've got to let me be a man and provide for you. I finally have someone in my life that I want, and I can do things for, you cannot just take that away, Angela. I take care of you, alright!"

She said, *"Alright, Damenian."* He said, *"Alright, Damenian." What* does that mean, Angela? She remembered her deceased husband, Booker, was the same way; he felt he headed the household, and his manhood required that he take care of the entire household.

She said, "Dame, it means I love you and I love being married to a beautiful man like you who can and wants to take care of me and our household".

With his arms around her and not pleased with the tone he spoke to her, he said, I'm sorry for my tone, baby. Are we okay? She said yes, I love you, Damenian. Immediately, he felt she was his angel and the best thing to ever happen to him. He lifted her chin upwards and said, "So we good, Angela? She nodded yes, he said, "So give me some sugar."

She kissed him passionately and warmly on his lips. Angela then asked him, "Is there a spending limit on this card, Dame?" Damenian chuckled while he headed to the door to go to work. She said, "Damenian, what if I spend over the credit limit?" He chuckled again and said, "Babe, trust me that won't happen." He then whispered under his breath, "Unbelievable, she's asking me *is there a credit limit, Damenian?"* He kissed her on the forehead, held the door open for her to exit for her appointment, and he to go to work.

Angela listened to Ms. Sonia and made an appointment to find out what was wrong with her. Angela went through a couple of routine tests before her doctor referred her to a GYN specialist. Angela was completely floored, caught totally off guard, and did not believe her examination could show she was pregnant. Angela could not accept her doctor's prognosis. She thought, how could she be? She's been married for only 5 months, so she would have therefore had to have gotten pregnant on her wedding night. She thought this was the 2nd marriage for both of them, no way, we would both have gotten pregnant during our 1st marriages.

So, Angela waited for her GYN specialist appointment scheduled for the next day. She didn't tell Damenian anything was going on; she felt she didn't need to tell him right now because there was nothing he needed to do. She also knew him and not telling him is a chance she'd be taking since he always wanted to know what was going on. She didn't worry about that; she knew she could handle Damenian if he found out before she told him. She would resort to her secret weapon and use it if it became necessary for him to see her cry.

Damenian cannot bear to see her cry, and she knew it. Angela needed someone she could talk to who also knew the power of prayer. In the meantime, Angela talked to God and went on a shopping spree with Damenian card.

After she returned home from her GYN specialist appointment, Damenian was at work, and she was home alone, trying to stay resilient with a clear head. She decided to call someone she loved and who loved her too. She fixed a cup of her favorite herbal tea, and she called "Mom" Damenian's mother. Damenian's mother is a faithful woman to the Lord, her church, as well as a praying woman. When Angela called, Mom knew right away something was wrong.

She felt Angela's spirit preceded her, always upbeat, full of energy, in love and happy, but that wasn't who was calling her. Damenian's mother knew something was wrong, so she said, "Angela, what is it! What's wrong?" Angela didn't want her to think something was wrong or happened to Damenian, so she said Mom, I'll tell you the quick version. Dame is fine, it's not about him, it's about me.

Mom, I'm pregnant. I found out today that it's for sure. I'm 5 months pregnant with a child and only married to Damenian for five months. Who gets pregnant on their wedding night! How! Who does that? I haven't said anything to Damenian yet because it's not a suitable time to tell him. He's working really hard on a huge project at work with his team, and I don't want to distract him from that.

He said they'll be wrapping it up soon, and he's planning to take me out, so I thought I'd just wait until then to tell him.

Angela said, "Mom, before you say anything, let me vent to you, please. I really need someone I can say this out loud to. Damenian takes me too fast. Mom, he proposed to me on our 1st date, he asked me to wear his ring and give us a chance, I fell crazy in love with him inside of 30 days just like he knew I would, oh I know now he knew I would, then I marry him in one year instead of the two years I wanted and on my wedding night I get pregnant, this is unbelievable. One last thing, Mom, I'm having a boy. I am going to give Damenian a son."

His mother broke her silence and said, "Angela, the night of your wedding, I remember distinctly I dreamed about fish, we know now who got pregnant. We can all see the love between you and Damenian, the way he looks at you, the way he says he loves you, the way you look at him, and how in love you are with him."

She continued, "It's not surprising you both created a life out of that love. Put your worries and your trust in God, Angela. One thing is certain: you and Damenian will be wonderful, loving, supportive parents, raising your child in the way he should go. I am so happy for him and for you. No more anxiety, you want to give your husband a happy baby, my dear, you must stop fretting and stay hydrated."

Angela said, "Thank you, Mom. I needed to hear that. I need a little time before I tell Damenian, so let's keep this between you, me, and Ava for now, because Dad and Myron would tell Damenian before I could tell him. I just want him to finish his project before I say anything to him. Well, Mom, 'Damenian Micheal Hammonds, Jr. III' is entering into this world in just a few short months."

Mom said to Angela, "I love you for giving my son a son and me my 1st grandchild. I'll keep fervent prayers over you, Damenian, and the baby." Angela said, "Thank you, Mom. I'll really need you with this one. Damenian's mother said, "Now get a glass of milk and take a nap, it's been a long day for you today." Angela replied, "Okay, Mom, I will. I love you," before she hung up.

Angela read her Bible and stayed resilient, just as Damenian's mother had advised. She read the story of Abraham and Sarah in the book of Genesis, and she immediately thought her pregnancy was God's promise to Damenian, like the promise to Abraham for a son with his wife Sarah for his faithfulness and obedience.

Angela asked in her thoughts, Why did God wait as long as he did for Damenian to conceive a child with her on her wedding night. Angela received this answer in her heart through the holy spirit. He waited until the time that there would be no question in anyone's mind that this was an act of God's power and Damenian's faith and obedience. Angela said, "Okay, I see you, God," and she took a nap.

Damenian had gone to his parents' home for a quick visit to help his dad with something he was working on without Angela because she didn't feel up for the ride. Mom asked Damenian to step into the kitchen for a moment before he left to go home.

When Damenian did, Mom whacked him with a wooden spoon. He said, "What was that for?".

She said, "Damenian, you brought Angela here to town Christmas before last on Christmas Eve; stayed here until the next day Christmas Day and you didn't come by to see your mother, your poor only mother who stayed in labor for more than 24 hours just to bring you into this world". Mom said, "I should whack you again Damenian". Damenian said, "Mom, how do you know about that". She said, "if you didn't tell me, guess who did."

He said, "Mom, I pursued Angela for 18 months, nearly 2 years, and she wouldn't go out with me. When she finally agreed to go out to dinner with me, I didn't have much time to prepare to ask her to marry me. I needed to take her somewhere so I could have her undivided attention on me, so I could shoot my shot, so I brought her here downtown. I didn't know how things would turn out between us. Actually, I kind of knew how things could turn out between us, but I wasn't 100% sure of that. I didn't want to bring her here to meet you until I was certain things would work out between her and I. As soon as I knew I had her, I brought her to you to meet her right away".

He said, "I'm sorry Mom, I know I hadn't come home as much as I do now that I have Angela, will you forgive me Mom". She kissed and hugged her son with both arms rubbing his back, knowing he didn't know yet he was going to be a father soon. Damenian said, "I love you, Mom, not everybody would have waited for up to 24 hours for me to come into the world the way you did". Mom said, "It was more like 5, maybe 6 hours, but I would have waited for you for 24 because I love you, Damenian". He kissed his mother on the cheek before he left to head home to Angela.

The day was their 6-month midway to their first wedding anniversary. Damenian and Angela were both filled with so much happiness. They were on their way to the dinner date trip Damenian promised her once the project was complete. They started their trip with a first stop for lunch with Damenian's parents. They hiked an exploration forestry trail near their home. The best sauerkraut hot dogs were to be had there if you hiked the trail to the commissary picnic area. They sat at a table for four outside on a beautiful sunny day. They were quite happy, carefree, laughing, talking, enjoying one another's company as they viewed the menu.

Damenian became distracted by a call from a member of the project. He excused his self, stepped away from the table, and paced while on the phone with one of the project managers. Angela whispered to herself, "I got to try, I got to try to get him." Angela walked over where Damenian was clearly getting frustrated with the person on the phone.

She stopped a short distance away from him and just stood there. When he saw her standing there, he placed his phone in his other hand and extended his free arm to gently pull her into him, where she rested her head on his shoulder, her forehead buried in his neck.

Damenian said to the person on the phone, "I need to care for my wife I'll have call to you back." Then Damenian said to Angela, "So you come over here to get me off the phone, huh"? Angela said, "No, I didn't, Damenian!!! I came over here to see if you needed some sugar." Damenian laughed and kissed her on those phenomenal lips of hers and again on her forehead, as they headed back to the table to order food.

While Angela placed condiments on her and Damenian's food, she asked him, "When are you going to step back from the project and give it to God Damenian? If you've done everything possible, you should not lose sight that it's been a long two months for some of us. Shouldn't your team go home and be with their families?"

Damenian listened to Angela's logic quietly before he said, "You're right." He called his assistant, Ms. Anita. He told Ms. Anita, "Get the team on a video call with me in 5," which means for them to drop everything, let me know when everyone, including you, is on the line. It took Ms. Anita 3 minutes to tell him everyone was on the video call.

Damenian began by thanking them all for their due diligence over the last 2 months. We will step back and step away from this project, meaning all hands are off. We've done everything possible to ensure this project moves forward and succeeds. There's no more left for us to do other than turn it over to a greater power than any of us. We're done, folks. Take the next few days and spend time with your families. I will be in the office next week, Monday morning, a little earlier than usual, to address whatever you throw at me.

Ms. Anita, yes, Mr. Hammonds, "you will no longer report to any member of this team, effective immediately." The support you provided the team during this project goes without saying. But, at the end of the day, you're my assistant and you'll return to your primary function as my assistant only. So, take off, spend some time with your family before Monday. Additionally, I will not be taking calls while I'm spending time with my family. Team, if you will, say greetings to the both Mrs. Hammonds and my Dad.

He turned his tablet around to allow them to see and greet Angela and his parents, something he had never done before. They all, one after another, expressed sincere greetings, and expressed it's truly our honor to meet them. Damenian then ended the call with, Enjoy your time off with your families because you all deserve it.

While the four of them dined on their meal, Angela knew it was time to tell Damenian she was pregnant. Angela didn't know how to start. He looked so happy, so she sat there silently. Damenian's mother saw she was struggling and stressed, finding how to begin. She helped her start by saying, "Angela, do you think it's time to tell Damenian, now?" Angela said, Yes, it's time to tell him.

Damenian froze dead in his tracks, looking at both his mother and Angela, trying to read their expressions before he said, "What?" He added, "Babe, what's going on, Angela?" He looked at his mother, who sat silently, and he turned to his father, who hunched his shoulders because he didn't know either. Damenian began to look stern in his demeanor. He sat back in his chair, took merely just one moment before he said, "Tell me what, Angela!" Angela broke her silence and said, "I love you, Dame." He said, "I know that, so tell me what?" She said, "Damenian, I'm having a baby." He looked at her, totally dazed and amazed, and ready to analyze every word about to be said.

His first question was. "How do you know that?" She said, "I went to the doctor to find out why I was sick every morning." He asked her, "You went to the doctor when?" She replied, "I went to see my regular doctor a month ago, and he then referred me to a GYN specialist because I'm pregnant.

Damenian stoned face asked her, "A month ago, Angela, and you're just telling me now?" She said, "Yes Damenian, I didn't want to distract you from the project at work. I felt I had time to tell you, but the time started running out. You needed to know whether you finished the project or not." The time started running out. "What does that mean, Angela?" he asked her.

She responded, "It means I'm 5 ½, possibly nearer to 6 months pregnant with your baby, Damenian." He said, "Are you sure about this, Angela?" She answered, "Yes, I felt the same way you're feeling when they told me. So, yes, baby, I am sure I am having your baby."

Damenian pushed his chair back and lowered his head between his legs for a few minutes. When he sat back up, Angela said, "There's more." His mother proudly watched her son's reaction; she was so happy and proud of him. Damenian said, "There's more; this isn't enough?" Angela said, "Yes, Damenian, there's more you need to know; I'm having a boy, I am going to give you a son, Dame."

Damenian put his head back down between his legs again and said, "Dad!" His Dad responded, "I love you, Damenian, and I'm so proud of you, son."

Damenian sat up again and was speechless, unable to say anything, his glassy eyes on Angela. Angela stretched her hand out to his hand, and she placed it on her baby bump and said, "Damenian, meet your son. "Damenian Micheal Hammonds Jr. III." She said to her baby bump, "Say hi to Daddy Damenian," and her baby bump kicked a couple of times for his dad.

Damenian said, "whoa, my son just kicked for me" Angela then took Damenian's dad's hand and placed it on the other side of her baby bump and said to her baby bump, Damenian, this is your granddaddy. He's going to be the best grandpa ever, and he's your daddy's best bud too. Her baby bump kicked a couple more times.

They found so much joy, laughter, and delight in that moment, in the gift of life given to them by God. Damenian and his father joked when he said, "Dad, you realize my son just demonstrated a Taekwondo kick?" His dad said, Damenian, you know, I think that felt more like a Jiu-Jitsu kick to me, son."

Ava and Myron called, asking Mom, did Angela tell him yet? Mom answered, "She did, he knows." Damenian asked, "Ava knew too?" Angela said, "Yes, she knew." Ava said, "Damenian, congratulations, brother, how do you feel?" He said, "I'm still processing it. I don't usually let people get close enough to catch me totally off my guard like this."

Myron interjected with a chuckle before saying, "Congratulations, you two lovebirds." "Thanks, Myron," Damenian then teased, "you realize you and Dad were asleep on the job over here. What happened, guys?"

Dad chuckled, "We didn't know they didn't tell us." Myron said, "If they told me, you wouldn't have been caught off guard like that, Damenian. You would have known something was going on; we would have told you something." Damenian said thanks, Myron. Angela said, "Only Mom, Ava, and I knew because if Dad or Myron knew, they would have told you before I had a chance to tell you." Ava added, "Damenian, seeing you surprised is priceless. Damenian shook his head and said, "I love you guys."

Damenian stood up, extended his hand to his wife, and excused his self for a private moment with her. Damenian and Angela strolled just a few steps away from the table. Damenian stood there in front of her, admiring her as if he was under a spell. He kissed her sweetly and tenderly with both hands clasping her face before he laid his head on her shoulder. She embraced her husband with both her arms, kissing him multiple times on his lips, cheek, and neck, as she held him.

Damenian broke his silence, placing his hand on her baby bump and said, "I have to cancel the trip, Angela. We'll need to head home. There's a lot we need to do and talk about since this news has completely changed our trajectory."

Angela said, " You're right, we need to head home, we need to talk, we need to figure out everything and begin preparing to be parents." She added, "I am so happy you know Damenian, so you can jump in to help make decisions." He said to Angela, "We'll be heading home soon, okay." Angela asked if they could stop by the dairy farm to get her a chocolate ice cream sugar cone and some fresh chocolate milk to take home. He said, "Absolutely," and began making the calls to cancel the reservations.

Angela's GYN specialist, Dr. Cooper, requested that Damenian attend her next appointment with him. Dr. Cooper needed to enroll them in birthing classes that would prepare them for labor, delivery, caring for a newborn, and most importantly, the postpartum depression period, which follows childbirth. Angela scheduled the appointment for Damenian and her to meet with Dr. Cooper in two days.

Damenian, Angela, his Mom, and Dad all hiked back to their cars. Damenian hugged his mother and said, "Thank you, Mom, I love you." He hugged his Dad, his face buried in his shoulder. Damenian lifted from hugging his father, patted him on the shoulder, and said, "They got us real good today, Dad, because you and Myron were napping on the job, you sleepy heads." They all laughed a good, hearty laugh before getting into their vehicles and driving home.

Once Damenian and Angela arrived home, they immediately noticed Ms. Sonia had left a congratulations card and a huge balloon that read, "It's a boy." Damenian asked, "Ms. Sonia knew too?" Angela said, "Yes, she knew before I knew. She said she dreamed about fish the night she met me, like mom did on our wedding night."

Angela ran herself a lavender-scented bubble bath with extra bubbles. She was so happy to be home and even happier that Damenian finally knew about the baby. Angela soaked while Damenian took a long shower, put on his PJs, and reclined in his reclining chair. Angela, feeling rejuvenated after she exited her bubble bath, she put on her PJs and curled up in Damenian's lap, where she fell asleep.

The next morning, Angela was up early, making breakfast while video chatting with Mom and Ava. She was glowing with excitement about Damenian taking her on a shopping spree for clothes to fit over her baby bump for church and everyday wear. When Damenian woke and walked into the kitchen, he was greeted by the aroma of jumbo shrimp in a herb and butter sauce, yellow stone-ground grits, crispy bacon, sausage patties, and Angela putting butter on a couple of toasted English muffins. He leaned in, kissed her softly, and said, "Good morning, babe. "Good morning, Dame. I love you, she replied, and he kissed her again and said, "I love you too".

Damenian then said, "Good morning, Mom, good morning, Ava. Tell Dad and Myron I hope to see those sleepy heads soon." They chatted for a while as Damenian began to fix two plates of food, one for him and one for Angela, while she finished up with the English muffins.

Angela asked Damenian if he wanted apple juice or orange juice. He said, "Apple juice," so she filled up two glasses. She sprinkled fresh, finely chopped cilantro over the top of their shrimp and grits with a slight sprinkle of smoked paprika for presentation. Mom said, "Now that looks delicious. Enjoy your breakfast, you two. I love you." They replied, "We love you too, Mom, and you too, Ava," before hanging up. Damenian reached for Angela's hands, as they bowed their heads, as he said the grace.

The following day was their GYN Specialist appointment with Dr. Cooper. That morning, Damenian made a toasted bran muffin with a bowl of Frosted Flakes for his breakfast while Angela got ready. Damenian and Dr. Cooper both quite enjoyed meeting one another; they blended nicely and instantly. Damenian could never take part in anything he did not research to make himself knowledgeable because that's who he is instinctively.

Dr. Cooper was more than impressed with Damenian, his knowledge, his use of the proper medical terminology, and his questions, especially his concern for his wife and the post-partum depression period. Dr. Cooper could sense clearly that Damenian wanted to be ahead of that for her. He wanted her to be safeguarded since she was no stranger to depression in the past, in her grief for her first husband, who succumbed to cancer in this life.

Dr. Cooper invited Damenian to follow him into the examination room, where Angela waited, so he could take a visual look at his son through the ultrasound. Damenian joked that's Angela's head for sure because my head isn't quite that big! They all had a hearty laugh. Dr. Cooper printed the ultrasound screenshot for them. Dr. Cooper felt quite satisfied with his meeting with Damenian. He always wanted to get a sense of what type of support would be in the delivery room with him. Dr. Cooper thought Damenian would be a great support for Angela.

After Damenian and the team brought the two-month project they worked so diligently on to completion, Damenian was offered the promotion of a lifetime. This promotion was the one he had worked so hard for over the course of many years. He immediately thought that this promotion, if it had been offered to him earlier, before so much had changed his life, would have been welcomed with far more excitement and agility.

This promotion at one time meant the world to Damenian, but he needed to be still and look at this opportunity in its entirety. The promotion he was offered would require him to relocate to California, and the amount of time he would be required to put in would nearly double. He now has a wife and a child on the way, and his family has been rejuvenated with joy since he married Angela. Mostly, he speculated because he had begun to come home more frequently than he had before Angela.

Ms. Anita was the first person to congratulate him. She's been his loyal assistant for more than 12 years, following him through numerous promotions as the only assistant he's ever worked with, and who he feels is partially responsible for his achieving this great executive promotion. Ms. Anita asked Damenian if she could have a moment with him after she congratulated him. She thanked him for the last 12 years and told him this new promotion was only the beginning for him, because after this, the sky would truly be limitless for him.

She stated she could not follow him into this new chapter of his career he worked so diligently to accomplish. She explained she would not be able to uproot her family for her selfish, ambitious reasons that would secure the job of a lifetime for her. Ms. Anita explained she loves her husband and her children too much to take them away from everything they know and love to start over in a new place and space they've never been to before.

She felt her family would possibly find themselves like fish out of water should they have to relocate to California, and she could not willingly put them in that position.

Damenian listened to her intently and quietly before saying to her It will be very difficult for him to make this move without her after 12 years of working together, carving the pathway to this, his dream position. He then said to her, "Ms. Anita, well-spoken, I truly understand your reasons for not being able to make this one last journey with me".

He asked her not to mention this promotion offer to anyone, since he, too, has to evaluate if it is going to be a good fit for his life now that so much has changed. She agreed to say nothing while he took his time to look at what would be involved in moving his wife and his newborn son to California.

Damenian did not try to mask or hide the fact that this was the offer of a lifetime for anyone his age. This new position that is being offered to him would definitely make the sky limitless for him in his future. The salary, the home they could buy, would be quite tempting and well deserved. Now, that is the bright side to this. So, he now needed a couple of days to look at the downside to the timing of this as well. He's been married to Angela for a little less than one year, and he unequivocally knew she would follow him wherever he had to go. So, he would need to uproot her from all she has known with a newborn child to a new state where she wouldn't know anyone, and she would see him far less than she does now. He considered whether she would feel alone due to his work schedule, how long she could be happy and continue to love him, even though, financially, they would have more than they have now.

He thought long and he thought hard about taking her away from their church and taking her away from his family who she has grown to love. He thought about his family, who are presently a two-hour drive away from them, which would turn into a plane ride away from them.

He factored in his mother and his sister, who are preparing to be first-time grandparent and aunt to his son, and how could he so calculatedly take that away from them? He thought about whether he should turn this opportunity down; someone who presently reports to him will be offered the career move of a lifetime, which he worked so hard for to earn.

He remembered once when he told the Lord he had everything he wanted and needed when he thanked God for what he had. He thought he would look at his situation, this promotion, and decide over the weekend and by Monday whether or not he'd be uprooting his newly acquired family to California.

Angela knew him; she could see something was weighing on his heart. She could see it in his silence; she could see him thinking it through. So, she kissed him passionately before she made passionate love to him in an effort to take his mind off of some of it. Actually, she didn't accomplish taking his mind off it, but she helped him make his decision.

He, too, like Ms. Anita, could not see uprooting Angela and their newborn son to a state she's never been to and where she'll not know anyone, while the majority of her time will be spent home alone. He could actually see that his marriage to her could possibly not survive for long. He realized he had everything he needed and wanted. So, he declined to accept the offer for this career move on Monday morning. Damenian thought, had it only come before him and Angela, how he would have been packed and ready to go before he had formerly got the offer.

Well, he's post Angela, and this promotion is just not as attractive to him any longer. To lose Ms. Anita, his Mother and his sisters' excitement for his first-born child outweighs the money and all the additional senior executive privileges to be gained. So, on Monday morning, Damenian officially declined the offer, and in doing so, he once again realized he really had everything he needed and prayed for.

Damenian's employer accepted his well-delivered reasons why he could not accept this tremendous career move at this time. So, his employer offered him to supervise, train, and have the new candidate continue to report directly to him since Damenian is clearly the best and only qualified person to handle this position. He accepted his new promotion offer to supervise directly the candidate who would be given the position he turned down. Damenian was given a hefty salary increase, without relocating his family. He immediately also gave a hefty salary increase to Ms. Anita for 12 years working seamlessly together.

As Angela and Damenian both began to focus on their baby's arrival, they both had such an awesome and wonderful time together purchasing baby items for their baby, their son. Angela decided to move her current office to another part of the house and make that her baby's nursery. She chose to paint the nursery a soft light powder blue. It was so beautiful and calming, you felt you were sitting in the clouds. After the paint dried, she walked around the room for inspiration on how to decorate for her son.

Angela had Damenian to get someone to stencil their son Damenian's name on the wall in rich royal blue letters with hints of silver highlights in an italic font. Angela purchased light blue and white animal-shaped rugs, as well as colorful stuffed animals and racing cars. She completed the nursery with furnishings and a crib. She and Damenian began shopping for baby clothes, diapers, bibs, receiving blankets, baby bottles, and other essentials for their son. Angela had Damenian purchase cases of high-quality, purified drinking water for their baby.

As time went on, they were the happiest they had ever been up to the moment when Angela's water broke. At first, she was confused by what had happened, so she called Ms. Sonia, who was in her new office down the hall, and she asked her, "Why am I so wet?" Ms. Sonia calmly called Mr. Hammonds, who was working in his office at home. She told him, "It's time, Mr.

Hammonds. Ms. Hammonds' water broke; you'll need to get her to the hospital."

Ms. Sonia helped with cleaning up Angela while Damenian called Dr. Cooper to tell him they were on their way to the hospital. Dr. Cooper said he's on his way, too. Damenian grabbed the bag Angela packed for her hospital stay and gently escorted her to the vehicle. He told Ms. Sonia to call his parents, tell them we're going to the hospital, and as soon as I get Angela settled in, I'll call them. Angela's labor pains were coming in intervals and began to come closer together. Damenian coached her to breathe through the intervals of her labor pain. Dr. Cooper came in to examine her and told Damenian we'll be taking her into the delivery room shortly.

Damenian had a white hand towel that he kept wet with cold water, and between her labor pain intervals, he gently patted her face and neck to rejuvenate her. Dr. Cooper came back for a second time and said to the orderlies, "Let's get her to delivery, now." Angela called, "Dame!" Damenian said, "I'm here, baby, I'm here; I'm not leaving you, so hold on tight to me, Angela. I got you." Dr. Cooper looked at Angela's vitals up on the monitor and realized Damenian had an ability to calm her. He thought the ability to keep her calm and alert to her environment was great.

Damenian talked to his wife while he cooled her down with the cold hand towel between labor intervals. He reminded her to breathe in cycles, just as they had practiced in birthing class. Dr. Cooper said, "We can see the crown of the baby's head. Push Mrs. Hammonds." Angela pushed as hard as she could, but it was not enough to push the baby out. Damenian cooled her down once again, rejuvenating her with the cold, wet hand towel. Dr. Cooper said to Damenian, "The baby's head is one and a half quarters out. Do you think you can get your wife to give a big, strong push?"

Damenian came close to Angela on her right side and said, "Baby, hold me tight, you need to dig deep down, use all you got to push, with all you got, baby push!" Angela squeezed Damenian's hand tight as she could and breathed like they were taught in birthing class. She pushed with everything, all she had inside of her; she did it for Damenian. She felt the baby when he exited from her body, and she said, "Dame, I did it." He said, "Yes, you did, Ange, you did it, baby, he's out." Damenian said, "I am so in love with you, Angela," she replied, "because I love you too, Dame."

Dr. Cooper spanked the newborn baby, and they all heard him cry for the first time. Dr. Cooper kept Angela and the baby in the hospital for a few days of observation before releasing them both to go home. Dr. Cooper told Damenian he did not find any signs of postpartum depression accompanying Angela's giving birth to their son. He also told Damenian, "The post-partum depression that follows childbirth has passed over your wife. She shows no signs of it, and I feel it's because of you".

Damenian said, "Because of me." Dr. Cooper said, "Yes, your wife loves you deeply and giving you a child is the greatest gift she could give you. Having your child brought her immense joy. Depression will not dwell where unimaginable joy exists because the two cannot co-exist. So, that Mr. Hammonds is because of you, and why the anticipated post-partum depression passed her over.

Dr. Cooper said, "Congratulations, Mr. Hammonds, you are a blessed man. Damenian looked at Dr. Cooper to acknowledge and receive his compliment of being blessed as he extended a firm handshake and said, "Thank you for all you've done for my family. God bless you, sir. Damenian brought Angela and the baby home from the hospital, and he enlisted plenty of help. Damenian had Ms. Sonia come in to help; his mother came to stay for a few weeks, and he had a nurse come daily. Damenian took-a partial leave from work, allowing him to work from his home office over the next few months, up to a year.

Angela loved the baby with her very being. She thought he was an amazing, beautiful little human. Angela would often pick her son up into her arms from his bassinet and curl up in Damenian's lap with him.

Soon Damenian was three months old, and he was such a happy baby with a tantalizing, infectious smile. Angela loved seeing her son smile and laugh. She was once on the bed playing with her child and a few stuffed animals, making both of them laugh with his infectious laughter. She looked up and saw Damenian standing in the bedroom doorway, watching her and his son laughing and playing with the stuffed toys.

Damenian, at 3 months old, lying on his back, saw his daddy standing there in the doorway. He began to flap his arms and legs so excitedly that he actually rolled his self over onto his stomach in the excitement.

That day forward, Damenian couldn't be left alone lying on the bed because he had mastered rolling over. Damenian soon began to crawl at 6 months, he was able to navigate in the baby walker at 9 months, and he was as curious as a two-year-old.

Angela often looked at her son and knew he carried Damenian genes. She could see him thinking, planning, and plotting something while he chewed on his pacifier rambunctiously. She thought she'd better watch this one, keep an eye on this little guy, because he was truly a busybody, a curious-natured baby who was very smart. Hence, she began to child-proof the house against his curiosity. Being able to navigate in a baby walker allowed him to get to things that could tumble down on him or could hurt him.

Before you knew it, Damenian was 16 months old and had a mind of his own; he was very smart and completely attached to his pacifier. Mom said Dame was also inseparable from his pacifier. Angela felt comforted knowing that.

They were an incredibly happy household of three attending church, with little Damenian dressed in a suit and tie. Many

Sundays, he was matching his dad's suit color with his pacifier in his mouth. Unlike Angela, Damenian no longer babied his son; he communicated with Damenian, knowing his son understood. Angela, on the other hand, looked at her son and saw her baby, whom she didn't want to grow up from being her baby.

One day, things changed when Angela made ravioli in tomato sauce for her son Damenian's lunch, adding seasonings and herbs to give it a little flavor. At the time, she was unaware that he didn't like tomato sauce when he tossed the bowl of ravioli against the wall. She had to feed him, so she gave him half of her tuna sandwich while she attempted to clean up the tomato sauce.

After he finished his lunch, she attempted to clean him up and to change his diaper when he squirted her while he laughed. He squirted her hair, her clothes, and the wall. She had enough of him and called Damenian, who dropped everything to come home.

When Damenian arrived home, the baby was in his playpen with stuffed animals, and Angela laid on the floor next to his playpen on a throw pillow. Damenian eyes immediately followed the squirt on the walls and the half-cleaned-up pasta sauce stains. Angela asked him not to touch her because the baby drowned her in the squirt. She got her shampoo and hair conditioner to wash her hair.

In the meantime, Damenian gave his son a baby bottle of imported water and told him to give him a minute to take care of mommy, and he would be right back for him. Damenian removed his suit jacket and wrapped a towel around his suit pants to function as an apron so he could help to shampoo Angela's hair in the kitchen sink while the baby looked on from his playpen. After he helped dry her hair with a towel, she began to apply leave-in hair conditioner. He ran her a bubble bath with lavender and extra bubbles the way she liked. Angela got into her bubble bath. Damenian ran for her and soaked.

He took his son out of the playpen so he could follow behind him while he changed his clothes. He began to address his son about what he had done to his mother today. He told his son these tantrums had to stop, treating your mother that way better not happen again. He said, "If you ever squirt her and laugh, you're going across my knee, buddy." While his son looked at him, understanding completely what he did felt wrong, his Dad further added, "I know you're just 16 months old and technically still a baby, but I have to factor in that you have the thought process of a 2-year-old.

You have to tell your mother you're sorry and let her know you won't do it again, bud. You've got to find a way to communicate with your mother. If you don't like something she makes for you, find your way to say no thank you, I don't want that, and do not throw it out of frustration. I'll talk to her about you're not liking tomato sauce, and from now on, you'll eat what we eat. No more of this baby food, okay, bud. Give me a high five."

Damenian picked up his son and carried him as he entered the bathroom, where Angela was soaking in the tub full of bubbles. Their son Damenian began to reach for his mother, calling her Ma, Ma. Damenian sat down on the floor next to the tub with his son, Damenian standing on his lap, calling for her. He started to have a tantrum, calling her Ma, Ma. She looked at her son and reached for him. His dad stripped his diaper off, and she kissed him and put him in the tub with her .

Damenian played in the bubbles while his mother and father talked. She found out her baby did not like tomato sauce, and she wasn't paying attention when he was trying to tell her. He told Angela he gets agitated if you or I don't get what he is trying to convey. We're his parents if we don't get him, who will, and that's what causes the tantrums. He said he found his way to tell you and me he doesn't like something or if he won't do it again.

He said Damenian, show mommy you don't like tomato sauce. He waved his hand and slowly shook his head back and forth. Angela laughed and said Okay, I'll know now. He said, "Tell Mommy you won't do it anymore." He put his hand up and briskly shook his head. They both laughed with pride as they developed communication with their son.

Damenian said, "The squirting simply better not ever happen again if I have to come home to help shampoo your hair, run you a bubble bath because my son squirted you, he'll be going across my knee, and that's for sure. Angela, he is growing up on you and me, although he is always gonna be your baby." Damenian said, "How bout I make dinner tonight? I'll make us a couple of smash burgers with cheese, and Angela, you can make homemade French fries with the Idaho potatoes."

Damenian got a towel to retrieve his son and assist Angela with exiting the tub as well. From this day forward, whatever Damenian ate for his dinner, his son Damenian ate the same. Damenian told Angela to pack a couple of bags, babe. "We're going to my parents' house for a few days. I'm taking you on an overnight dinner date, just you and me, so bring a dinner dress." Damenian said to Angela, "Mom said they are so excited to have Damenian for a few days. She said pack him a hoodie because they'll be going to a couple of dads' sunrise martial arts training sessions, and some mornings are a little chilly".

Damenian tends to evaluate his son's capability to communicate without throwing tantrums. Once, while they were at his parents' house, he told his son, "Damenian, go tell your Ma to come give me some sugar". The baby took off running to the kitchen, pushing his mother and saying cum, cum. While his grandaddy and Uncle Myron spied to see whether he could do it. Angela asked him, "Did Daddy tell you to come get me?"

He nodded his head, Yep, and continued to push her towards the den where Damenian was. Once in the doorway of the den, she said, "Damenian, did you tell the baby to come get me?".

Damenian said I told him to tell you to come give me some sugar. The baby continued to push her leg, saying cum, cum. Angela went over to Damenian and kissed him passionately on his lips before she rested her head on his shoulder.

The baby then came over with both arms stretched, and both his parents lifted him into Damenian's free arm, where he too laid his head on his daddy's other shoulder. Damenian's dad took a picture of them with his phone and said, "I am so proud of you, son." With their eyes upon Christ, they lived, loved, and were blessed beyond what they could have imagined.

After Damenian spent quality time alone with Angela on an overnight dinner date, he made plans to soon take his wife and son on a family trip to the Sesame Street Theme Park in Philadelphia, Pa., for a few days of amusement park fun and festivities. Damenian, at the time, was still 16 months old and completely fascinated with the Sesame Street theme park environment and the colorful characters he watched on TV every morning without fail.

While at the theme park, Big Bird, Elmo, the Cookie Monster, and other characters walked around and would stop to take a picture while holding small children, who mostly cried because they were frightened of them.

When Big Bird approached Damenian, who was in his father's arms, he reached for Big Bird to hold him. While he was in Big Bird's arms, Damenian was fascinated by the idea of exploring inside Big Bird's mouth while he rapidly chewed his pacifier. He was actually very curious and quite interested in putting his head in Big Bird's mouth. Damenian had to literally pull his son out of and away from the mouth of Big Bird. Damenian had to do it again; he had to literally pull his curious son out of the mouth of the Cookie Monster, too. Elmo didn't want to take a chance with picking up little Damenian; he opted just to shake his hand instead and take a picture with both him and his dad and avoid his curious exploration of getting inside his mouth.

Angela had been a little under the weather during the trip. So, when Damenian and the baby headed out to the amusement park on day 2, she went to the pharmacy inside their hotel. Angela purchased a pregnancy test kit, and it came back positive. She went back and purchased a couple more home pregnancy test kits, and they all came back positive that she was pregnant. She got rid of all the tests and headed out to meet with Damenian and their son while she contemplated her next move.

Angela learned her lesson when she was pregnant with her son to never keep anything like this from Damenian again; he'll have to be the first to know, unequivocally. In the meantime, she wanted only to see Damenian and her toddler son both happy and enjoying themselves like they were, because to see them happy filled her with great happiness and joy. So, she decided to wait until she got home to make an appointment to see Dr. Cooper, her GYN specialist, who delivered Damenian, her son.

After spending 3 days in Philadelphia, Pa., at the Sesame Street Theme Park, they returned home feeling rewarded and rejuvenated to have spent family time together in such a fun place. Angela scheduled an appointment to see Dr. Cooper once she arrived home. Dr. Cooper confirmed she was indeed pregnant again, approximately 4 and a half months. At first, Angela expressed concern that Damenian may be disappointed with her or think she's irresponsible to have gotten pregnant again. Dr. Cooper, sensing Angela's dismay with herself and the news, tried to encourage her.

When he said to her It's a girl, Mrs. Hammonds, she said, "What?" Dr. Cooper repeated, You're having a girl," Angela lit up like a Christmas tree. She thought, what woman on earth wouldn't love to have a daughter? Immediately, she began rejuvenating herself in happiness, delighted by Dr. Cooper telling her she is having a little girl, a daughter. She thanked Dr. Cooper and said she would tell Damenian tonight.

Dr. Cooper set an appointment for her and Damenian to meet with him in 2 weeks. At which time Angela would be 5 months with child, so he could enroll them both in child birthing class. Angela, unable to contain her excitement, was extremely happy that she was pregnant with a little girl. She was ready to tell her good news to everyone only after Damenian knew first.

When Angela arrived home, Damenian was packing for an immediate departure on a business trip internationally for a couple of days. His immediate attention was needed in their Dubai location he oversees. Damenian asked Angela if she would help him pack for at least a 3-day stay. She began laying out everything he needed before she packed it into his suitcase while smiling with each thought she is having a little girl.

Damenian was packed and ready to head to the airport, but before he could leave, Angela said she had to tell him something. He said, "Alright, what is it?" She said Damenian, I'm pregnant, I'm having a baby. He said, "What, you're what? Another baby?" She said, "Yes, Damenian, I'm having another baby." He said, "Are you sure about this?" She said, "I saw Dr. Cooper this morning, and he confirmed I am 4 and a half months pregnant. Evidently, the birth control method I chose to use didn't prevent your daughter from getting in."

Damenian said, "My daughter," Angela said, "Yes, your daughter, I'm having a little girl, Damenian, and I am so happy about that." Damenian gently pulled her in and hugged her with both arms. He said, "I am happy too, Angela, as long as you promise to stay in your element of happiness while you are carrying our second child." Angela promised she would.

Damenian headed off to his business trip while he and Angela both shared the news that they are expecting their second child, a girl. Angela's pregnancy was different this time than when she carried Damenian. The combination of swollen ankles and morning sickness made the pregnancy intriguingly different.

Damenian and Angela met with Dr. Cooper and were enrolled in birthing classes. Dr. Cooper addressed Damenian's questions and concerns to the best of his ability regarding his wife's safety, having another child in the small span of 2 years. Once Dr. Cooper and Damenian concluded their discussion, they headed over to the examination room where Angela waited.

Dr. Cooper did an ultrasound so both Angela and Damenian could see their daughter, who had a head full of hair. Dr. Cooper stated that's why the nausea and morning sickness you're experiencing is so tough on you, your daughter has so much hair. I'll have to give you something to help you with the nausea.

It was that very moment, while looking at the ultrasound image of his daughter, Damenian fell hopelessly in love with her and thought she was going to be the exact spitting image of Angela. They knew the routine, so they were back at it again. Angela prepared a princess-themed nursery for her daughter. She had such a great time purchasing pink outfits, ribbons, and all the girlie things needed for Angelina. Angela named their daughter with Damenian's consent and blessing "Angelina Damiana Ava Hammonds. Whenever Damenian, the father, and his son talked to her baby bump, which was regularly, Angelina would kick up a storm for both of them.

Angela's water broke early one afternoon. Ms. Sonia called Mr. Hammonds; it's time to take Ms. Hammonds to the hospital; her water broke. Damenian called Dr. Cooper and headed to the hospital with Angela. She remained in labor for upwards of 9 hours before Dr. Cooper told the orderlies to take her into the delivery room. Damenian remained by her side, talking to her, encouraging her, and rejuvenating her through the process.

After a long and tedious labor, Angelina was born. She, unlike her brother, came out crying. Angela was so exhausted that she fell into a drowsy-like sleep while appearing to be awake. Dr. Cooper said she's experiencing Post- Partum Depression, and all we can do at this point in time is to wait for her to come out of it. We must just wait.

Damenian stayed by her side both day and night for days; he wouldn't leave her. He spoke to her, he read to her, he prayed for her, and he waited for her.

Angela was in a place where there was no color; it was just gray. She remembered this place; she was here before Damenian came, when she lived in grief. When she was here before, she didn't have what she carried with her and stands on now, and that is the word of God. She took the word of God, and she formed a Battle-Axe with it. She knew the word of God was able to free her, and she was ready to battle what was trying to keep her there. So, she meditated with the word of God while she waited on God for the hour to free her.

None of this was easy for Damenian. On day 3, he asked his mother and Ms. Sonia to stay with Angela so he could go home for a little while, to change, hold, and pray with his son. Once home, Damenian prayed fervently with his son for his wife to return to their small family; he beseeched God that he and their children needed her. At that exact moment, Mom and Ms. Sonia, on each side of Angela, holding her hand, formed a circle.

They both began praying and lifting up the name of almighty Jesus in unison. Angela, wherever she was, could hear them, so she closed her eyes to receive what God was gonna do. Mom and Ms. Sonia both continued to pray fervently over Angela, filling the entire atmosphere with the power of the holy spirit. Suddenly, they both began to speak in many foreign tongues in unison, they both began being filled up with the grace and mercy given to them by God at the exact moment Damenian wiped a tear and said Amen.

While there in the room with Angela, Mom and Ms. Sonia spoke life into Angela by speaking the word of God over her, telling her to get up!

Suddenly, Angela's lunch tray began trembling; it trembled until a cup of hot water for tea popped up, turned over, and spilled, untouched by human hands. Angela, wherever she was, opened her eyes, sat up, and said Mom, Ms. Sonia is Dame and Damenian, alright.

Damenian's phone rang, and it was the hospital. He answered the call. This is Damenian, the nurse on the other end confirmed that he was Damenian Hammonds. He said yes. She said I was told to call and inform you that there has been a change in your wife's condition, and you should come, sir, right away. Damenian said, "Okay, I am on my way. He placed his son in the vehicle in his booster seat, and they headed to the hospital. While carrying his son, Damenian entered Angela's room and froze in his tracks to his surprise. Mom and Ms. Sonia were in the room, happy and joyous, with Angela, who was sitting up in bed holding their daughter, Angelina.

Angela said to her son Damenian, Come give mommy and your new sister a kiss, he headed to the bed, where Ms. Sonia removed his shoes and helped him to climb up so he could kiss his mother and his new baby sister.

She looked over at Damenian and said, "You okay"? He didn't look okay to her; he looked like he needed a good night's sleep, as if he hadn't slept in days. He couldn't answer her; he just looked at her with glassy eyes. She said, "Come here, Baby," and patted the other side of the bed. Mom and Ms. Sonia said, "We're going to give you both some time together, and we'll be in the café if you want us."

Damenian came over to Angela, kissed her on her forehead, and climbed on the bed next to her and said, "Welcome back, sleeping beauty." She said I thank God and the word of God for bringing me back.

She kissed him on his lips and gave him his daughter to hold and bond with, while she cradled her firstborn, their 2-year-old toddler, in her arms. Damenian looked at their daughter, Angelina, and said, "Babe, she is so beautiful, and look at all her beautiful hair, it's just like yours." Damenian, with the pride only another man could understand, looked at his wife and their 2 children, and he was grateful.

Angelina Damiana Ava Hammonds was a happy and active baby. At 7 months old, she could scoot and navigate a baby walker. Angela could see Damenian genes clearly as she watched her daughter chew her pacifier rambunctiously while plotting, planning, and thinking it through, unlike her brother. Damenian genes in his children is something else Angela thought.

When they were enjoying the Steak dinner Angela made, Damenian age 3 and Angelina 12 months old. Damenian told his mother and father he felt he wasn't getting enough physical exercise. Angela felt concerned and said, "well I thought you get outside time at preschool for that, so the children could play and run". Damenian said, "we do mommy, but I want more it's not enough I want real exercise. Damenian his dad sat silently listening to the conversation between his son and Angela his mother. He recognized the conversation because he too had this same conversation with his parents when he turned 5 yrs. old and now his son is going after it at age 3. Damenian listened intently as his son and Angela talked.

Angela said, Damenian I know you are just a 3-yr old toddler so honey what do you suggest daddy and I should do? She said, "son after I care for you, daddy and your sister it doesn't leave me with much time for much else.

Since I love you so much what will you have your mommy to do? I will find time and the energy to do what will make you happy so you can use up some of that untapped into energy you feel you need to burn". Damenian said, thank you mommy, I love you mommy, all I need you to do is say yes, say okay for daddy and granddaddy to start my training. I'm ready mommy to start my martial arts training.

Daddy and Granddaddy, they won't train me unless they know you said it's okay, I can start. Angela said, I don't know about this are you sure Damenian this is what you want to do. Technically, you're still a baby, I mean, you're only 3 years old, and you're still my baby. I don't know, I need time to think about this. Angela at that very moment realized Damenian, her husband, hadn't said a word; he merely listened and never interjected his opinion or a suggestion.

Angela looked at her husband Damenian who was looking and waiting for her reply to their son. She looked at her son who began to pick at his dinner while he waited for her response to him, then she looked over at her daughter Angelina who was eating having the best time enjoying the Tomahawk Steak dinner Angela made with no interested in their conversation at all.

Angela said to her son, "Damenian it's Yes, it's okay with me. You have my blessing to begin your martial arts training with daddy and granddaddy, make me proud, son". Damenian said, I will mommy I promise, then he said, Daddy will you train me? Damenian said with glassy eyes, yes son I will because I can see you're ready; so, I'll call your grandpa after dinner and let him know. He said to Angela, baby I love you; Angela responded pointing her finger at him and she said, he's my baby Dame so no broken bones, alright!

Damenian smiled, chuckled as he shook his head and said, "you really watch way too many kung-fu movies, but none the less, yes maam I promise your baby will not come back to you with broken bones".

Damenian then said to his son, I'm proud of you son and I love you! Damenian said, I love you too Daddy. After dinner Damenian went into his home office to video chat with his dad. He told his father about his son's desire he expressed at dinner this evening to begin his training.

Damenian father told him to call his son into the office so he could question Damenian in an effort to validate if he's really ready at the tender age of 3. After they both questioned and listened intently to his response to their questions Damenian's grandfather proclaimed you're right he's ready son. So, they both setup the day and time they would begin training Damenian in Taekwondo and in Brazilian Jui-Jitsu knowing he would be the youngest to be trained in both of these arts.

Damenian since he was 16 months old attended many of his grandfather's training matches and well knew his grandfather was "Kwan Jang Nim" a high rank in martial arts meaning his grandpa was a "Grand Master" earned by many years of experience and training. Damenian, at a very young age, knew what would be involved to earn his martial arts belt colors. Dad said Damenian you know he'll possibly earn his gray belt by or before his 4th birthday in Brazilian Jui-Jitsu.

Damenian said, Dad, he could also possibly obtain his yellow belt in Taekwondo at the same time by or before his 4th birthday. Damenian father said, "let's get him uniformed and into his white belt so we can both start his training, Damenian said, okay Dad.

The White belt*: signifies in Brazilian Jui-Jitsu and in Taekwondo the symbolism of innocence and ignorance, a new beginning of a student's lack of knowledge. It is the commitment to learning discipline for foundational techniques.*

The Yellow belt*: signifies the foundation of Taekwondo has been laid signifying the earth from which a plant sprouts and takes root the yellow belt is earned after the white belt enforces dedication and commitment to the art.*

The Gray Belt*: in Brazilian Jui-Jitsu for children, signifies developing, understanding of fundamental techniques, control of positions and the relevance of discipline and respect that is earned after the white belt.*

At the tender age of 3, Damenian began martial arts training on Saturdays. He trained in the morning with his father in Taekwondo and he trained in the afternoon with his grandfather in Brazilian Jui-Jitsu.

An entire day spent among three generations training in the discipline of the martial arts. Angela particularly loved having Saturdays to herself and her daughter, Angelina.

She'd get up early, fix Damenian and her son breakfast, before they head out for a day of martial art training exercises. She would then spend her day with her 12-month-old daughter, Mom, and Ms. Sonia shopping, lunching, and doing girlie things.

While all had been going well for Damenian and Angela, the devil was plotting to come against them to destroy the happiness God granted them. After all these years, after all this time, Damenian's ex-wife (Clara) was now showing up to create havoc and gloom upon Damenian and Angela's marriage. There was no good reason for her to show up, other than to harass Damenian at this point and time in his life. She decided to come into their lives at this time, realizing he was happy, content, and feeling blessed.

Damenian once claimed he had all he wanted and needed when he prayed to thank God for what he had. Angela not only threw him a lifeline when he needed it after a very bitter divorce, but she also gave him two children in the process. His life with Angela is a life he never knew with anyone before her. He often thinks about how they never argue and fight, how they always talk things through. They had their fair share of silent disagreements but never heated fights and screaming matches like he had with his ex-wife, Clara, whom he thanked God Almighty she was gone.

It was during this time that Mom and Ms. Sonia found out Clara had been making numerous failed attempts to get to Damenian (thank you, Ms. Anita), so they both jumped into action. Damenian had taken Angela and his children on an international vacation, which made his ex-wife's frugal attempts to contact or reach him useless. Ms. Sonia and Mom intercepted Clara's message to Damenian. So, when she showed up expecting to be meeting with Damenian, it was with Mom and Ms. Sonia instead, to her complete horror and surprise.

Mom gave her one warning and said to her, "You will get away from my son and his family, you low-life-Jezebel". Mom said he is happier than I can remember seeing him. He's in love with his wife, he has children with her, and because of that, you have no place here! You want my son; do you really want my son? Then you'd better be ready to go through me to get him!

 Mom immediately, intentionally struck a Jiu-Jitsu martial art pose and said, "Come on!!! And get this spanking, you filthy, unclean witch".

Ms. Sonia said, "Now wait one minute here, please. I didn't put these Converse sneakers on today for nothing, ladies. So, baby, before you go over there to go through Mrs. Hammonds, you're gonna first need to go through me to get over there, you ungodly heathen. Mr. Hammonds is a good man, a hardworking, God-fearing man who loves his wife and children. You have no business here, you she-devil. Baby, let me tell you, you'd best leave here right now and never, we mean never, try to contact Mr. Hammonds again. See, baby, this way you go now, Mrs. Hammonds won't have to Jiu-Jitsu kick your behind, and I won't have to cut it, you getting any of that? Mr. Hammonds doesn't do shanky women like you anymore now that he has Angela."

Clara said, "I'm so sorry" Damenian's mother said, "Your sorry excuse for finding redemption in someone else's husband is unforgivable. My son will never be that for you. Stay away from him and stay away from my family. Now get out of here!!!" Clara left very quickly, in tears, and never attempted to contact Damenian ever again.

Damenian and Angela never knew what had happened, and they never found out. Mom, Ms. Sonia, and Ms. Anita never told them. Because they were so happy and in love with each other, they all felt that telling them would be a horrible distraction for no good reason. So, they decided to say nothing to them about it; they decided to let them keep their eyes on God and each other while they handled it for them.

God continued to bless and favor Damenian, Angela, and their toddler children. Damenian now 3 years old, and Angelina 12 months old, looking every bit like her mother, Angela. They were a loving, close-knit family of four. Damenian led his family to serve the Lord, as he protected, provided, and cared for them. He loved his family and felt truly blessed by having them.

One day, while Damenian was at work, Angela called him, sounding a little frantic when she said, "Dame, don't get upset or excited, the baby and I are fine." Damenian their son had begun preschool, so he was in school on this day. Damenian said, "What's happening, Angela?" She told him a strange man had been following her for the last three days when she was out. She said, "I have no idea who he is and why he's following me." Damenian said, "Where are you!" She said, "I am parked one block away from your office." When I noticed he was back and following me again, I drove to you. Look out your window, do you see me? And directly across the street from me is the guy in the silver car with tinted windows.

Damenian said, "I see you and him, make sure your doors are locked, now drive into the employee parking lot, baby, while I watch you. At this time, Damenian was in the parking lot circling on foot, ready in anticipation.

The silver vehicle made a U-turn to follow Angela. Damenian said, "Come on, baby, take your time, he's following you." Damenian told gate security to open the gates wide and not to let anyone entering see you. He shouted, "Just duck!" He said, "My wife will be in the first vehicle, the white Cadillac SUV behind her will be a silver car with tinted windows, don't let this guy see you.

I want this character to think she's entering the parking lot all alone and unattended. Once that silver car follows my wife's vehicle into this parking lot, close those gates; no one is to enter or exit. I primarily want that silver car's exit blocked with no way out," They said, "yes, Mr. Hammonds."

Damenian walked through the parking lot and told Angela to park in his reserved parking space, where he had security to escort her and his daughter to his office until he got back. Damenian walked up from behind the silver parked car and reached into the driver's side window, turned the ignition off, and removed the key. He then opened the driver's side door, and the guy was caught by utter surprise when Damenian hit the seat belt release and dragged the guy out of the car toward the dumpsters.

Damenian lifted the guy up by his throat off the ground into the air. Holding the guy in the air off the ground with one hand, he said to him, "Why are you stalking my wife? How long have you been following my wife, man?"

The guy began to cry and plead with Damenian not to hurt him or kill him. He said, "I knew her when she first started a business a few years ago". Damenian thought that this guy was a little on the wimpy side for this, so he dragged him back to his car and placed him in the driver's front seat, both feet on the ground. Damenian said, "give me your driver's license," and took a picture of it with his phone. He said to the guy, "you don't live near here, so why are you following my wife in this community?" The guy began by explaining to Damenian that his name is Chandler."

(Note from the author: If you read volume I, then you know who Chandler is from p. 18-19).

Damenian leaned against the car parked directly across from the guy's car and listened intently as the guy went on to explain to him. He said, "He had no idea or any way to have known she had gotten married."

He further added, "She began a business and would bring packages to be mailed at the shipping store where I worked as a counter clerk. I thought we were liking each other, and I thought we sometimes flirted and smiled at one another, at least I thought we were.

All of a sudden, she stopped coming to the store. No good-bye, no nothing, she just never came back anymore. About a week ago, I saw her. I approached her to say hello, but she didn't recognize or remember me. I could see clearly, she's out of my league. So, I said nothing, I just left, and I started following her. I guess it was stupid, but I hoped to get the nerve to say something to her, but I could see she was just being polite back then and not actually into me."

Damenian continued leaning against the car parked adjacent to him with his sleeves rolled up, arms folded, ready to start questioning him. After a lengthy line of questioning, Damenian was satisfied that this guy got in over his head and had never done anything like this before.

He called Ms. Anita, who was in the window the entire time, so afraid for the guy because she knew Damenian Hammonds very well; she worked as his assistant for more than 12 years. Following him as his assistant through his many career promotions. So, when it comes to his family, she didn't know what he would do.

He asked Ms. Anita to get Art Kinson out of San Diego on the phone, and would you please get my daughter a fruit cup or something from the cafeteria? She said she already did that, Mr. Hammonds, he said, Thank you, Ms. Anita.

Damenian answered, "Artie, it's been a long time. Art said I owe you still, Damenian, for everything you've done for me, my family, and my life. Damenian said you did the work to make it all happen; I just moved an obstacle or two out of your path. So, what do I owe for this call?" Damenian said, "I have an employee of yours in one of your local supply stores here near me. He's been stalking my wife when she has been out with my child for about a week."

Damenian said, "I have that all under control; he met her briefly before she dated and married me, and her hands aren't completely pure in any of this. She may have innocently flirted with this character at one time, nothing serious. Anyway, I want this guy transferred to one of your San Diego locations.

I believe he's making minimum wage here, which won't sustain him or his family when he moves out there. So, I want him to be given a $20 an hour wage increase over his minimum wage salary so he will stay there and far away from here. If he leaves there for any reason, I will be clear with him that I will crush him, so I'll check on him from time to time.

If he leaves San Diego, I'll promise him he won't find employment anywhere, and I mean absolutely nowhere, because I will personally shut him down. He stays in San Diego, he'll be in a position to send for his family, earning $27.89/hour, he'll be able to provide for them."

I want him to report to his new employment location in 48 hours at the hourly rate we just discussed. I want his current job terminated in exactly 48 hours as well, when he's expected to begin working at the San Diego location." Damenian said, "I hope he uses this opportunity I am giving him, as you did, and builds on it from there. Send this guy a letter of relocation with a report to start work in 2 days, starting at the $27.85 hourly wage, and send me a copy of that letter.

I have him here with me right now, and I am going to go over with him what's about to happen. Damenian said, "Thanks, Art, I owe you. Yes, the family is fine. I had a second child, a little girl, yes, sir. She's the perfect likeness of Angela; my Mom and Dad are fine, still doing their sunrise Jiu-Jitsu thing. Will do, take care, God bless."

Damenian was clear with Chandler never to set foot back in this State again because there's nothing here for you. He kicked his shoe over to him and told him to be in San Diego in 48 hours, or hell will become your new lifestyle. He then told gate security to let him out.

Back in his office, Angela had a playpen blanket spread on the floor with a doll and stuffed animals she kept in a small toy chest in the closet in Damenian's office for her children. She asked him, "If he handled it," he replied, "I did." She asked him, "why was the guy following her?" Damenian said, "His name is Chandler." he watched for her reaction when he told her he worked for a shipping company as a counter clerk.

He thought he knew you from a long time ago. She said, "Before you, I had only been with Booker until he died. I have never been with any other man in my life except you." Angela asked him, "Will he stop following me now that he knows I am not who he thought I was?" Damenian said, "he won't be following you anymore; he'll be moving out of state in a couple of days."

She said, "that is wonderful. I need to head to the grocery store for dinner before I pick Damenian up from preschool." He said, "I'll wrap up things here and take you and my daughter where you want to go." Angela said, "I thought you said you took care of it, Damenian." He said to her in a tone, "I did"!

It will be a long while, Angela, before you and my kids go roaming around without me after today. Do you think you can just call me and tell me some guy has been following you and my daughter for days? It's been handled, Angela, but it'll be a long while for me to process that call. I will be taking you and my kids where you want to go, Alright!"

Angela said, "Yes, alright, Damenian, I understand." Damenian at this exact moment realized more than ever before that his job was to protect, keep his family safe, close, and happy; exactly what he did for many years to come.

Art Kinson contacted Damenian and said Chandler had shown up for work and appeared to be working out just fine. He had already sent for his parents and his girlfriend to join him in San Diego. God had blessed every member of his family to find jobs and a delightful home they could afford.

It was an extraordinarily long time before Damenian trusted Angela and his children to go out without him or Ms. Sonia. Damenian had firmly put his foot down on this and he did not budge.

The years passed so quickly, before you knew it, both children were attending high school, and before you knew it, they were both off to college. For the first time since they were married, Damenian and Angela finally had their house alone to themselves, just the two of them. Remember, their son, Damenian, was conceived on their wedding night.

Now that the children were off to college and gone, Damenian purchased the big black 4x4 monster pickup truck he wanted but had to put on hold because he was a family man with small children. And now he could finally walk around his house in his birthday suit, as nude as a Jay-bird if he wanted, now that they are gone.

Angela was finally able to gut and remodel the kitchen now that there would be no children living in a construction zone. And she was finally able to play her R&B throwback music as loud as she wanted; now they were gone since they couldn't play their music loud.

Ms. Sonia got married to her Boo, Mr. Pete, who pulled the numbers at Wednesday afternoon bingo. They both attended the Hammonds family Thanksgiving and Christmas dinner each year as part of their family.

Damenian parents continued sunrise Jiu-Jitsu martial art training five days a week, where any member of their family who needed them could always find them.

Chandler remained in San Diego for the duration of his life, never leaving, feeling blessed to be there and able to provide for his family.

Ava and Myron had twin boys, giving Mom and Dad a total of four grandchildren, making Damenian and Angela first-time uncles and aunts as well as first-time Godparents to their children.

God has a way of blessing those who seek and keep their eyes on him. He not only blessed the entire Hammonds family for their faithfulness and obedience to raise up their children in the way they should go, but everyone who crossed their path was genuinely blessed as well.

A Note from the Author:

This is where we'll end our look into their journey after the wedding in Volume I. Thank you, God bless you for reading Volume II of this amazing story.   Who knows, perhaps there could be a Volume III in the future that will let us see their children grow up, become teenagers, and go off to college. We know what we know, and that is Damenian will fight hell in high water for Angela and his children. Thank you again for reading!

God Bless,
Inez Shack-McRae, author